ABOUT THE BANK STREET READY-TO-READ SERIES

More than seventy-five years of educational research, innovative teaching, and quality publishing have earned The Bank Street College of Education its reputation as America's most trusted name in early childhood education.

Because no two children are exactly alike in their development, the Bank Street Ready-to-Read series is written on three levels to accommodate the individual stages of reading readiness of children ages three through eight.

○ *Level 1:* GETTING READY TO READ (**Pre-K–Grade 1**)
Level 1 books are perfect for reading aloud with children who are getting ready to read or just starting to read words or phrases. These books feature large type, repetition, and simple sentences.

○ *Level 2:* READING TOGETHER (**Grades 1–3**)
These books have slightly smaller type and longer sentences. They are ideal for children beginning to read by themselves who may need help.

○ *Level 3:* I CAN READ IT MYSELF (**Grades 2–3**)
These stories are just right for children who can read independently. They offer more complex and challenging stories and sentences.

All three levels of The Bank Street Ready-to-Read books make it easy to select the books most appropriate for your child's development and enable him or her to grow with the series step by step. The levels purposely overlap to reinforce skills and further encourage reading.

We feel that making reading fun is the single most important thing anyone can do to help children become good readers. We hope you will become part of Bank Street's long tradition of learning through sharing.

The Bank Street College of Education

To Caroline Bunn
—W. H. H.
In memory of my mother,
Carmella Trotta
—A.T.T.

THE MONSTER FROM THE SEA
A Bantam Book/November 1992

Series graphic design by Alex Jay/Studio J

Special thanks to James A. Levine, Betsy Gould,
and Diane Arico.

Library of Congress Cataloging-in-Publication Data
Hooks, William H.
The monster from the sea / by William H. Hooks ;
illustrated by Angela Trotta Thomas.
p.   cm. — (Bank Street ready-to-read)
"A Byron Preiss book."
"A Bantam little rooster book."
Summary: A determined princess, whose father's policy
of keeping strangers off their island kingdom
has made her curious about the outside world,
finally gets her wish to meet someone new.
ISBN 0-553-08951-X. — ISBN 0-553-37024-3 (pbk.)
[1. Princesses—Fiction.]   I. Thomas, Angela Trotta, ill.
II. Title.   III. Series.
PZ7.H7664Mo   1992
[E]—dc20
91-39365   CIP   AC

Published simultaneously in the United States and Canada

Bantam Books are published by Bantam Books, a division of Bantam Doubleday
Dell Publishing Group, Inc. Its trademark, consisting of the words "Bantam Books"
and the portrayal of a rooster, is Registered in U.S. Patent and Trademark Office
and in other countries. Marca Registrada. Bantam Books, 1540 Broadway, New
York, New York 10036.

Bank Street Ready-to-Read™

The Monster from the Sea

by William H. Hooks
Illustrated by Angela Trotta Thomas

A Byron Preiss Book

BANTAM BOOKS
NEW YORK • TORONTO • LONDON • SYDNEY • AUCKLAND

Once upon a time,
not so long ago,
a princess lived
on a faraway island.

Her father, the king,
wanted to keep everything
just as it was.
So he never let any strangers
come to the island.

Her mother, the queen,
liked it that way.
All of the people on the island
liked it that way, too.
Everyone did—except the princess.

"I want to see new people.
I want to visit new lands,"
she cried.
"Your father would never
allow it," said the queen.

One day a fisherman
came running to the castle.
"Help! Help!" he shouted.
"A monster came out of the sea!"

"What kind of monster?"
asked the princess.
"A long black monster
with slimy skin
and big webbed feet,"
said the frightened fisherman.

Everyone in the castle
rushed to hear the fisherman.
"I would like to see the monster,"
said the princess.
"No, no!" shouted the fisherman.
"The monster has an evil eye
right in the middle of his head."
The king warned his people,
"Don't go near the sea!"

But the princess hated
being locked in the castle.
She longed to go to the sea
to look at the monster herself.

That week, no one dared
go near the sea to fish.
Soon there were no fish to eat.
The people grew hungry.
But they feared the monster
with the evil eye.

One day when everyone
was hiding behind closed doors,
the princess slipped out of the castle
She took her horse
and rode down to the sea.

She searched the quiet shore
looking for the monster.
But all she saw was a
small boat.

Suddenly the monster popped
up from the sea,
with his big evil eye
shining in the sun.

He walked up on the shore
with his huge webbed feet
flapping on the sand.
The princess was afraid
of the black slimy monster.
But she did not flee.

Then the monster did
the strangest thing.
He reached down and
pulled off his huge webbed feet.

He reached up and
pulled his big evil eye
away from his head.
He looked at the princess
and said, "Hello."

"Hello!" said the princess.
"You're not a real monster!"
"No, I'm not," said the stranger.
"My name is Jason.
I'm a scuba diver.
Haven't you ever seen a wet suit?"

"No," said the princess.
"My father never lets strangers
come to our island."
Then she laughed.
"We thought you were a monster!"

"That's why everyone ran
when I came ashore,"
said Jason.
"My boat is broken
and I need help.".
"Come, Jason," said the princess.
"My people are fishermen.
They know all about boats."

Jason jumped on the horse
behind the princess.
As they rode to the castle,
Jason asked,
"Why weren't you afraid of me?"

"That's simple," said the princess.
"I just wanted to see
what a monster looked like."

When Jason and the princess
reached the castle,
the king was happy to learn
that there was no monster.
And he was curious
about Jason's wet suit.

"It must be magic," said the king.
"You can breathe underwater.
What a remarkable man you are!"

By the time his boat was fixed,
Jason and the princess had grown
very fond of each other.
"If you will marry me,"
said Jason,
"I'll stay on this island."
"I will marry you,"
the princess answered,
"but *not* if we stay.
I want to see the world
beyond this island."
When the king heard this news,
he said,
"You will never be happy
unless you go.
So go with my blessing."

Soon Jason and the princess
were married.

To this day
they go scuba diving
all over the world.
But they come back
to the island
every now and then.

And the king loves to hear
about all the wonderful things
they see.

He also likes to have
a stranger visit, now and then.